W9-COT-041

Everything You Need To Know About

YOUR LEGAL RIGHTS

Every individual has certain rights that can never be taken away.

• THE NEED TO KNOW LIBRARY •

Everything You Need To Know About

YOUR LEGAL RIGHTS

Kenneth Fox, Ph.D.

THE ROSEN PUBLISHING GROUP, INC.
NEW YORK

Published in 1992 by The Rosen Publishing Group, Inc.
29 East 21st Street, New York, New York 10010

First Edition
Copyright © 1992 by The Rosen Publishing Group, Inc.

All rights reserved. No part of this book may be reproduced in any form
without written permission in writing from the publisher, except by a
reviewer.

Printed in the United States of America

Library of Congress Cataloging-in-Publication Data

Fox, Kenneth.
    Everything you need to know about your legal rights / Kenneth
Fox.
        (The Need to know library)
    Includes bibliographical references and index.
    Summary: Briefly discusses the legal rights of individuals,
emphasizing real-life situations in which teenagers may find
themselves.
    ISBN 0-8239-1322-8
    1. Minors—United States—Juvenile literature. 2. Civil rights—
United States—Juvenile literature. [1. Law. 2. Children's rights.
3. Civil rights.] I. Title. II. Title: Your legal rights. III. Series.
KF479.Z9F697   1992
342.73'085—dc20   91-13340
[347.30285]   CIP
                                                              AC

Contents

Introduction

*B*obby came home from school and slammed his book bag down on the kitchen table.

"I don't understand my new history teacher," he said to his mother. *"She told us about something that happened before the American Revolution, when the states in the United States were still colonies of England. The king of England appointed the governors of the colonies. If the governor didn't like what you were doing, he could have you arrested.*

"She told us about a newspaper editor in New York City. He printed some stuff about the governor of New York, and they arrested him and put him in jail.

"Then they had a trial. The newspaper editor said the laws didn't give the governor the right to lock people up for things they printed in newspapers. The jury agreed with the editor and let him go free."

"So what don't you understand?" Bobby's mother asked.

"Well, the teacher asked us what we thought," Bobby said. *"I said that people are supposed to obey the law. If the law is bad, they should get it changed. But if people just went around breaking laws they didn't like, everything would get crazy."*

"What did your teacher say then?" she asked.

"She said I was wrong, but I had a right to my opinion," Bobby said. *"That got me even more mixed up. How can I be right when I'm wrong?"*

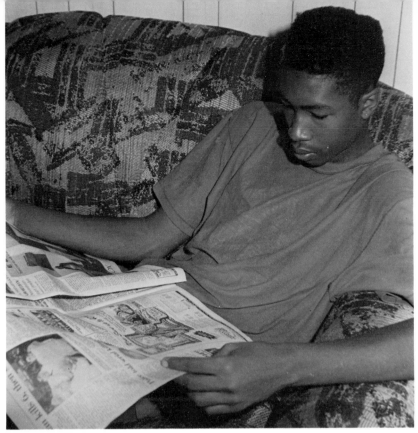
Freedom of the press allows people to publish their opinions openly, without control by the government.

"She was talking about your <u>rights</u>," his mother said. "The newspaper editor had certain rights and you have rights, too. Everyone has rights."

"Are rights different from being right?" Bobby asked. "Do I have a right to be wrong? I need a map or something to figure all this out."

The Right to Freedom of the Press

The newspaper editor Bobby's teacher was talking about was John Peter Zenger. He claimed he had the right to *freedom of the press*. This meant the government could not control what he printed in his newspaper. Since his trial, all Americans have enjoyed the right of freedom of the press.

"Even your school newspaper is protected," Bobby's mother said. "The principal cannot interfere with what the writers say. She cannot prevent them from printing an article she disagrees with. Not even if the article criticizes her."

"I don't believe that!" Bobby exclaimed. "What if she's right and the criticisms in the school paper are wrong? What happens then?"

Your Rights and the Legal System

Legal systems and governments are based on laws. Laws are written to tell what is right and wrong. When someone breaks the law, he or she is usually thought to be doing something wrong. But sometimes people do not agree about what actions are wrong.

In the United States and Canada, the legal system also includes *rights*. The right to freedom of the press and to freedom of speech are two of those rights. These rights may be written down in an official document, but they do not have to be.

Our rights are based on our beliefs about freedom and equality. The *Declaration of Independence* explains part of the story when it says: "We hold these truths to be self-evident: that all men are created equal; that they are endowed by their Creator with certain inalienable rights; that among these are life, liberty and the pursuit of happiness."

The American Revolution was a war to win independence from England. It was a war to win the rights expressed in the Declaration of Independence.

Soon after the American colonies won the war, the *Constitution* was written. The Constitution explains how the United States government is organized and how its laws are written.

The Constitution had to be approved by the people before it could go into effect. Many people did not like the fact that the Constitution did not include statements of their rights. They agreed to approve the Constitution, but only if government leaders promised to include *amendments* (additions) that spelled out people's basic rights.

This promise was kept. Within a few years, ten amendments were added to the Constitution. These ten amendments are known as the *Bill of Rights.*

The Legal Rights of Young People

"Do kids get these rights too?" Bobby asked his mother. "Men and women may be created equal, but adults get to do lots of things kids aren't allowed to do."

"You have the same rights adults have," his mother explained. "The difference between adults' rights and kids' rights has to do with being able to use your rights.

"Having rights also means having responsibilities. If you aren't mature enough to use your rights responsibly, your use of your rights must be supervised. You may not get complete use of all your rights until you are older."

Everyone, regardless of age, has the right to rally support for a particular cause.

Chapter 1

Young People's Rights: Protection and Limits

*J*anine Givens and her friend Lee Palmer are 11 years old. They live in Andover, Massachusetts. When they had a report to write for school, they went to the public library.

They found only a few useful books in the children's section, so they went to the adult section. The librarian told them they had to be 12 to be allowed in the adult section. She made them go back to the children's section.

Janine's mother became upset when she heard what had happened. She tried to find out whether the girls would be allowed in the adult section if they had their parents' permission.

She found out that the library rule applied to all children under 12, whether or not they had their parents' permission. The purpose of the rule was to make sure adults were not disturbed.

11

Asserting Your Rights

Janine and Lee decided the library rules were keeping them from exercising an important right: the right to read. They decided to do something to get the library to change its rules.

They circulated a petition asking the library to change the rule. The petition was signed by 150 children. Local newspapers learned of the petition and printed stories about it. A large color photo of Janine and Lee holding the petition appeared in the Sunday paper.

Janine's mother and other parents said that they supported the petition also. They did not think the library had a good reason for its rule. They recognized that there were reasons for limiting young people's rights. But they did not think the library should limit their children's right to read.

Reasons for Limits on Your Rights

Everyone enjoys the same rights. Adults may exercise their rights fully. As a young person you possess the same rights, but your use of those rights can be limited for three important reasons.

• Protection

The first reason is the need for protection. Your parents have a legal responsibility to protect and care for you. In order to do this, they may limit your rights.

Your local government can also limit your rights to protect you. For example, some towns have curfews requiring young people under age 16 or 14 to be off the streets after 10:00 p.m. These curfews are meant to protect you from danger or prevent you from getting into trouble.

Some parents make many rules and punish their children for breaking these rules. They believe rules are an important way to protect their children from harm. If your parents are very strict, you may think you have no rights at all. But this is not true. Your parents can protect you by limiting your rights, but they cannot take your rights away completely.

• **Lack of Maturity**

The second reason for limiting young people's rights is their lack of maturity. Young people's powers of reasoning are not fully developed. They are often not able to separate what is good for them from what is harmful.

The PG-13 restriction on many movies states that children under 13 cannot see the movie unless accompanied by a parent or guardian. This restriction shows how limits are lifted as young people become more mature. If you are 13 or older, you are considered mature enough to see PG-13 movies without parental supervision.

Restrictions on young people's right to vote are also based on their lack of mature judgment. You cannot vote until you become 18. Until 1971, the voting age was 21. It was reduced to 18 because most people had come to believe that 18-year-olds were mature enough to vote responsibly.

• Conflict with Your Parents' Rights

The third limitation on young people's rights arises from conflict with the rights of their parents. One of the most important rights of parents is the right to decide how their children will be educated. Another is the right to determine their children's religion.

If your parents think that certain books will interfere with the way they want you to grow up, they have the right to prevent you from reading those books. In some towns, the public library keeps young people from borrowing certain books when their parents request such restriction.

You *Can* Fight City Hall

While your rights can be limited, you should never feel that your rights can be taken away.

"You can't fight city hall," people often say. They are wrong. We have the rights we have today because people throughout our history have stood up against rules and laws they believed were wrong. They fought city hall and won.

Andover's library officials are considering whether the policy should be changed. Janine and Lee are waiting to see if their petition has succeeded. If you lived in Andover, would you sign Janine and Lee's petition? Are children restricted from the adult section of the library in your community?

Chapter 2

You and Your Parents: Parental Abuse and Other Violations of Your Rights

Your parents have a special relationship to you where your rights are concerned. They have the right to determine many things about how you are brought up. They have the right to determine where you will live, how you will dress, and where you will go to school. They even have the right to prevent you from being friends with someone.

As we learned in Chapter 1, all rights include responsibilities. Your parents' rights carry with them parental responsibilities. Your parents have a responsibility to provide a good home for you. They must see that you get an education. If you are sick, they must get medical care for you. Also, they must never hurt you physically.

If your parents do not carry out their responsibilities, they are committing a crime. They can be arrested and put in jail. If they still do not care for you properly, the legal system may take you away from them. Another family would then be found to take care of you.

Abuse

Leona came to school one day with a large black and blue mark on her leg. Her teacher asked what had happened. Leona said she fell on the ice outside the school.

The teacher sent Leona to the school nurse. The nurse asked Leona how she hurt her leg. Leona said she fell on the stairs. The nurse called Leona's mother.

When Leona's mother arrived at the school, the nurse told her to take Leona to the hospital. The doctor at the hospital took an X-ray of Leona's leg. The X-ray showed Leona's leg was broken. It also showed where her leg had been broken several years before. The doctor asked Leona's mother when this had happened. Leona's mother said she did not know the leg had been broken.

The doctor suspected Leona was a victim of parental abuse. Parental abuse is a legal term for serious injury done to a child by the child's mother or father.

The doctor called the state Department of Child and Youth Services. When the caseworker from this department arrived, she took Leona from the hospital

Every child has a right to be properly cared for by parents or legal guardians.

to her office. A police officer came to take Leona's mother to the police station. Later the police officer went to Leona's house and arrested her father.

Leona was very scared and very sad. The caseworker asked Leona if her father had broken her leg. Leona began to cry again. She said she loved her father and did not want anything bad to happen to him.

Many children are abused by their parents. Leona is not the only one. Often the only way to protect abused children is to arrest the parents who have hurt them. Leona's father spent the night in jail.

The next day, the judge allowed Leona's father to return home. The judge ordered that the whole family must receive counseling. Once a week they all went to a counselor's office. Discussing the problem with the counselor and the family helped Leona's father. He learned to control his anger and not hurt Leona.

Neglect

One of your rights is the right to be supported and cared for by your parents. If your parents do not care for you well enough, they are violating your rights in another way. They are guilty of *neglect*. Sometimes children are neglected because their parents need to be away from home a great deal. Sometimes parents cannot buy food or clothes because most of their money goes to pay the rent on their apartment.

Neglect does not always mean that the parents are deliberately doing something bad. They may be trying as hard as they can. They are just not able to make everything work out.

Often parents do not know about programs that can help them. *Medicaid* is a government program that will pay for a visit to the doctor or a stay in a hospital if your parents cannot afford to pay themselves. *Food stamps* are available to help pay for groceries. There are also programs to help pay part of the rent on apartments.

What to Do If You Think You Are Abused or Neglected

Your parents are the people you turn to first when you need help. If your parents are the ones causing the problem, you may not know where to turn. The best thing to do is to talk to someone you trust. There may be a teacher at your school that you like. You may have a friend whose mother or father you can talk to. If you are on a team or belong to a school club, you may be able to talk to your coach or sponsor.

The most important thing to remember is that what is happening to you is NOT YOUR FAULT. You have a right not to be abused or neglected by your parents.

is the legal separation of two married people. Often, one of
nts is given custody of the children.

Chapter 3

When Parents Separate and Divorce

"*D*ear Diary," *Joanna wrote in her secret book. "Mom and Dad have been fighting again. It makes me so sad. I wish they would love each other again."*

Joanna's parents had been fighting for more than a year. Things were not getting better. Joanna's father threatened to move out.

"Dear Diary," Joanna wrote two weeks later. "This morning Dad screamed that he was leaving and never coming back. I ran to my room and slammed the door. Dad tried to get me to come out but I wouldn't."

That night Joanna's father did not come home from work. The next morning a man delivered a letter to Joanna's mother. Joanna asked her what it said. Her mother said it was about a meeting they were going to have with some lawyers.

Separation

The special letter Joanna's mother received was from the lawyer representing Joanna's father. Joanna's mother also hired a lawyer.

At the meeting, they discussed an agreement for *separation*. Her parents both signed the agreement. They agreed to live in two separate places.

Joanna and her mother would continue living in the house. Joanna's father would live somewhere else. Joanna would stay with her father every Wednesday night and every Saturday and Sunday. He would give Joanna's mother part of the money to pay for the house, food, and other things.

Divorce

Joanna's parents agreed that they would live apart for six months. Then they would decide what to do next. When the six months had passed, they decided to get a *divorce*.

In a divorce, two married people get legal permission to stop being married. They must go ask a judge in court to give them permission.

If there are children, the judge decides who shall have *custody* of them. Custody means living with and caring for them. It is being responsible for what happens to them.

Joanna's parents asked the judge to approve *joint custody*. For Joanna this meant she would spend part of the week with her mother and the other part with her father.

The Best Interests of the Child

When parents separate and divorce, there can be a problem about who will take care of the children. Often both parents want complete responsibility. They don't want the other parent to have anything to do with the children.

When this happens, the legal system steps in. A judge listens to each parent. The judge may ask the children what they want. Then the judge decides what shall happen to the children. The judge must determine what is best for the children. Sometimes the parents don't get exactly what they want.

The judge may give the parents joint custody of the children. Other times, one parent may be given custody. In these cases, the other parent may have *visitation rights.* These rights tell when and where that parent may visit the children.

Sometimes one parent does not do what the judge ordered. The father may stop paying for the children's expenses. The mother may move and not tell the father.

If your parents are divorced, they do what was decided in the divorce agreement. If they don't, they are committing a crime. They can be arrested and put in jail. The laws about divorce are strict. They guarantee one of your most important rights: the right to be cared for.

Our compulsory education laws mean that children from age 6 to 16 must go to school and must have the choice of a free education.

Chapter 4

Do I Have to Go to School?

"*I* hate school," *Ramone complained as his mother shook him awake. "Why do I have to go to school? We never learn anything. All our teacher ever says is 'Be quiet! Get back in your seat!'"*

Compulsory Education

Going to school is one of your legal rights. The constitution of your state provides that you have the right to a free education. These laws are called the *compulsory education laws.* They provide that all children from age 6 to age 16 must receive an education.

Compulsory education laws were passed around 100 years ago for two reasons. The first reason was to prevent parents from forcing their children to go to work. Before, parents had the right to send their children to work instead of to school. These laws gave parents the responsibility of making sure that their children received an education.

25

The second reason for these laws was to make cities and towns build school buildings and hire the necessary teachers. Before the laws were passed, cities and towns often failed to raise the money to build the new schools that were needed.

Public Schools, Parochial Schools, and Private Schools

Your city or town is required to make sure there is room for you in the *public school* system. But you do not have to go to a public school. Many children attend *parochial schools* run by churches and religious groups. Other children attend *private schools* with no religious connections. Most of the money to run these schools comes from the parents of children who attend them. Cities and towns do not pay for the education of children attending parochial or private schools.

Your Rights at School

Janna and Peter wrote an article for their school newspaper about the baseball team. They charged that the four best players were not attending any of their classes. When the principal saw the article, he ordered that the papers not be given out. He removed Janna and Peter from the newspaper staff.

When Janna's mother heard what had happened, she called the principal. He told her the article could keep the baseball team from playing in the state championship game. The principal said he was trying to protect the school and the team.

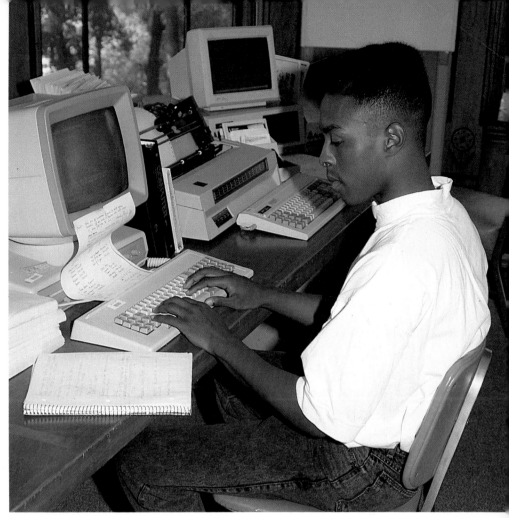

Most printed material—including your school newspaper—is protected by freedom of the press and the right to free speech.

If Janna and Peter had been reporters for their town newspaper, the principal could not have interfered. The rules for students writing for a school paper are no different.

The rights to freedom of speech and freedom of the press apply to student reporters and school newspapers. Principals and teachers may not remove a student from the staff. They cannot prevent the newspaper from being distributed because they do not like what the student writes.

Child labor laws say that a person must be at least 16 years old in order to work legally.

Chapter 5

What If I Want to Work?

*P*erry is 13, but he is very tall for his age. He got a job at a gas station pumping gas from 3 in the afternoon until 11 at night. The station wasn't very busy in the evening. He had time between customers to work on his school assignments.

One afternoon a caseworker from the state Department of Labor came into the station. She asked the manager, Mr. Sawyer, whether Perry was old enough to be working in a gas station. He told her Perry had said he was 16.

The caseworker asked Perry whether he had a work permit. Perry said he didn't think he needed one. The caseworker said he must tell her how old he was. She was very serious. Perry knew he had to tell her his real age.

Child Labor Laws

The caseworker told the station manager he was in violation of the state's child labor law. She told Perry he would have to get a work permit. "Even with a permit," she said, "you will not be allowed to work in a gas station. The law prohibits young people under the age of 16 from working in gasoline stations and other places that are considered dangerous."

Compulsory Education and Child Labor: Two Laws that Work Together

Child labor laws were passed about 100 years ago. This was at the same time state governments passed their compulsory education laws. The two laws work hand in hand. The education laws make parents and schools see that every child is provided with an education. The child labor laws make parents and employers see that children work only when they are old enough and only under suitable conditions.

If you were working in violation of the child labor laws, you would not be penalized. Instead, your parents and the person employing you would be considered at fault.

The child labor laws also protect you from doing work that is dangerous. Perry cannot work in a gas station while he is under 16. The lawmakers in his state believed working in a gas station was dangerous for someone of that age.

There is one kind of dangerous work that young people under 16 are allowed to do: harvesting fruit and vegetables. Legislators in farm states believe that depending entirely upon adults for harvesting would cost too much money. The prices of the fruits and vegetables would be too high. Customers at the supermarket would not buy them.

Your Rights at Work

When you do work, you are protected by certain rights. You have the right to be paid for all the work you do. You have the right to be paid the *minimum wage* per hour. Minimum wages are set by Congress and by state legislatures.

You can find out what the minimum wage is in your state when you apply for a work permit. Usually work permits can be obtained at your school. If not, someone there should be able to tell you where you can get one.

Getting a work permit is important. You must have a permit to defend yourself if your rights at work are violated.

Work and School

Some young people feel that the education laws and the child labor laws *prevent* them from exercising their rights. They want to be left alone to quit school and go to work. Your rights are restricted until you are 16 for your protection. The laws protect you now and when you are 16 and older.

"Hanging out" in most public places is usually okay, unless it violates laws against loitering or creating a nuisance.

Chapter 6

On the Corner and at the Mall

*J*erome and Al live on Morris Avenue, up the hill *from their school. Tony, Ed, and Lou live down Morris Avenue in the opposite direction. After school they like to hang around on the corner before heading home. They joke about what happened that day. There may be some shoving and yelling.*

Mr. Banks owns a drug store on the same corner. Many of his customers are elderly people. They are afraid of the boys. They wish Mr. Banks would do something to stop the boys from hanging out in front of his store.

The police tell Mr. Banks that they understand his problem. They explain to him that the boys have a right to be in front of his store. The police say they can only tell the boys to move away if they are creating a nuisance.

One Person's Right Can Be Another Person's Nuisance

The legal definition of a nuisance is the same as its everyday definition: a thing or activity that interferes with someone's enjoyment, causes them physical discomfort, or makes them afraid they will be injured. These meanings are easily understood.

The problems arise when there are differences of opinion. Mr. Banks's elderly customers say the boys make them afraid. The boys insist they have a right to be on the corner. They say that they are careful not to bother Mr. Banks's customers.

Who is right? Should Mr. Banks be allowed to have the police tell the boys to move? Should the boys be allowed to continue hanging out at the corner? Also, who should decide who is right? Will the boys, Mr. Banks, and Mr. Banks's customers all have to go to court, with their lawyers, and ask a judge to decide the matter?

The best solution would be for the boys who are claiming their rights and the people who are bothered to try to come up with an answer. This might happen if the police arrested the boys and everyone went to court. Then the judge could tell everyone concerned to get together and work things out.

"Under Eighteen Not Admitted Without Parent or Guardian"

Almost everyone knows a store that refuses to let kids under age 18, or 16, enter by themselves.

Usually it is the kind of store that sells things kids like. It may sell gum, comic books, candy bars, games, records, or tapes. If you have been kept out of a store, you may have asked yourself: "Don't I have a right to go into any store I want?"

The law does recognize a person's right to shop, but it is a right that can be restricted in some ways. Owners of stores can legally prevent young people from entering. What they cannot do is allow some young people to shop but not others.

A store that allowed white kids to shop but not black or Hispanic kids would be violating the *civil rights* laws. These are laws prohibiting different treatment of people because of race, sex, physical handicap, and some other reasons. We will hear more about civil rights in Chapter 11.

Shopping Malls: Public or Private?

Shopping malls raise more complicated questions about rights. A mall is actually a very large building. Inside the building are stores similar to the stores along a street. The owners of these stores can restrict who enters. There are also open areas inside the mall. These are known as *common areas*. Legally, common areas are like city streets and sidewalks. They belong to everyone. The mall owners cannot prevent anyone from entering the mall and using these common areas.

If you have visited malls with your friends, you may have had difficulty exercising your right to walk or stand in these common areas. A mall security officer may have warned you that you will have to leave the mall if you cause trouble. You may have been told that it is illegal for more than three or four of you to stand or walk around together.

Is it legal for malls to make their own rules and force you to leave if you break a rule? Many lawyers and judges would answer "No." When the mall owners invite everyone to come into the mall, the walkways become *public property.* This means the mall owners must allow people to do all the things they have a right to do on the streets and sidewalks outside the mall.

Getting mall owners to agree not to make special rules for young people is difficult. Can you do anything about the rules at the mall you like to go to? It will not be easy. It would help to have your parents and your friends' parents request a meeting with the mall owners, the mall security officers, and the police chief and mayor or chief administrator of your town.

Such a meeting could show the mall owners that you and your friends are serious. It could show that you understand that rights come with responsibilities, and that you take your responsibilities seriously. The mall owners and security officers might be surprised to find that young people know so much about their rights.

Chapter 7

Sex and the Law

*S*ue and Chuck are in love. They sit by themselves
in the school cafeteria talking softly to each other.
After school they hide under the stands at the football
field. They hold their breath and kiss as long as they
can. Some of their friends have "gone all the way,"
but Chuck and Sue worry about having intercourse.
They don't want Sue to become pregnant.

They also know that intercourse can give you
AIDS. They had a special class in school about
sexual abuse and sexually transmitted diseases. Nei-
ther one of them has had sex before, so they don't
think they can give AIDS to each other. Still, they just
aren't sure. If you are worried about AIDS, you can
read about it in another book in the Need to Know
series: Everything You Need to Know About AIDS.

Your Sexual Rights

Your sexual rights are restricted until you are
considered mature enough to exercise them freely.
Young people mature at different ages, but states
must set an official age for sexual maturity. This
age is called the "age of consent." It is 18 in many
states, but younger in others. Until you reach this
age, it is officially "against the law" for you to have
sexual intercourse.

Age of consent laws are very old-fashioned. For
example, most consent laws apply only to the girl.
They do not set any age of consent for the boy.
This is because some consent laws were written to
please fathers. Fathers wanted the legal system to
punish anyone who had sex with their daughters
without their permission.

The boy or man who violates the consent law is
guilty of *statutory rape*. Rape occurs when a person
is forced to have sex against her will. *Statutory* is a
legal term. It means that a person is guilty of a
crime because someone involved is younger than
the age stated in a law.

A boy or man is guilty of statutory rape if the girl
with whom he had sexual intercourse is younger
than the age of consent. He can be found guilty and
punished *even if the girl consented to having intercourse*. Until she reaches the age of consent, the
law restricts a girl's right to make her own decisions
about sexual matters.

People over the age of 18 have the legal right to "consent" (agree) to sex with others over that age. Everyone—no matter what their age—has the legal right to refuse sex with anyone for any reason.

Your Rights if You Become Pregnant

When Sue's friend Amanda became pregnant, she went to a family planning center to get help. The counselor at the center suggested she have a blood test to be sure she was pregnant. Amanda told the counselor she didn't know what she would do if her father found out.

Amanda's test showed she was pregnant. She asked the counselor whether she could get an abortion. An abortion removes the developing egg from a woman's uterus. This ends her pregnancy.

The counselor explained that every woman has the right to end a pregnancy through an abortion. In some states, restrictions apply to young people. Some states require that girls obtain their parents' permission before having an abortion. Other states require that the girl's parents be told, but do not require the parents' permission.

Abortions and the Law

On Sunday evening, for no apparent reason, Amanda began to cry. When Amanda got control of herself, her mother asked her what was wrong. Amanda told her about getting pregnant, and her appointment for an abortion.

Amanda's mother was very glad Amanda had told her about what had happened. She told Amanda a very deep secret. When she was 17, she had an abortion too.

"Abortions were completely illegal in those days,"
Amanda's mother said. *"I had it done in a doctor's
office. It cost $300. My three girlfriends helped me
raise the money.*

*"The doctor's instruments weren't clean enough,
and I got an infection,"* Amanda's mother said. *"My
temperature went up to 105° and I almost died.*

"Since abortions were legalized," Amanda's
mother reassured her, *"doctors can do them safely in
hospitals or clinics. The danger of something going
wrong is very small."*

The Right to Life and the Right to Choose

Up until about 20 years ago, it was illegal to have
an abortion in every state in the United States. The
Supreme Court gave their opinion about this. They
gave their answer in a very important case called
Roe vs. Wade.

The judges did not say that women have a right
to end a pregnancy through an abortion. What
they said was that ending a pregnancy is a *private*
decision.

The Supreme Court judges said that government and the law cannot interfere with people's
private decisions. Pregnant girls and women, along
with everyone else, have a *right to privacy.* One of
the things this right allows them to do is end a
pregnancy by having an abortion.

Women's right to privacy also allows them to prevent pregnancy by using birth control devices. These rights are often called the *right to choose* or the *right of choice.* They refer to a woman's right to choose whether or not she wants to have a child.

Most people agree that there is such a thing as the right to privacy. Many people do not agree that pregnancy and abortion are entirely private. They believe that a baby comes to life at the moment a woman becomes pregnant. They insist that this baby has a *right to life.*

The supporters of the right to life want abortions to be made illegal again. They claim that when an abortion is performed a baby is being killed. They say abortions must become illegal to guarantee the right of these babies to live.

Your Right to Have Your Baby

Until a few years ago, a girl younger than the age of consent who became pregnant and had her baby could have the baby taken away by the legal system. Today you have the right to keep your baby in almost all cases.

You have the right to continue going to school and to bring your baby to school with you. Your school must help you take care of your baby while you attend classes. Sometimes all the mothers and their babies are together in the same classroom. The babies sleep or play while the mothers take part in classes.

Chapter 8

Drugs and Alcohol

*M*artha and Laurie were doing their homework at Laurie's house. Laurie's mother and father were at work.

"I know where my dad hides the key to the liquor cabinet," Laurie said. She got the key and opened the cabinet.

"You try this one," Laurie said, "and I'll have some of this. It smells like oranges."

"That's really sweet," Martha said. "Let's have some more of that."

"Don't have too much," Laurie said. "It makes you feel really funny."

When Martha got home she did feel funny. Her mother asked her what she did at Laurie's house.

"Were you doing something you shouldn't at Laurie's house?" her mother asked. "You look sick. Did Laurie give you liquor to drink?"

"Well, we only had a few sips," Martha said. "I didn't think it would hurt me. I guess liquor is stronger than I thought."

"Drinking can be dangerous. You have to be careful, especially at your age," her mother said.

Regulation of Alcohol

In most states, it is illegal to buy alcoholic beverages until you are 21. Until recently, some states had 18 as the *legal drinking age.* This is the same age at which young people can vote and exercise other adult rights. But with the rise of alcohol-related car accidents the age was raised to 21.

Your parents may allow you to drink at home under their supervision. Restrictions are necessary because alcohol, even in small amounts, can distort your judgment. Even for adults 21 and over, drinking is restricted. No one may drive a car if they have drunk more than a moderate amount.

Drugs: Legal and Illegal

Many drugs are regulated because they also can distort your judgment. They interfere with your ability to do ordinary tasks like driving a car.

Many drugs that doctors prescribe are dangerous. They can only be purchased at a drugstore with a prescription signed by a doctor.

You probably also know about illegal or "hard" drugs such as marijuana, cocaine, crack, and heroin. The laws against these drugs are very strict, partly because the drugs are distributed and sold by large networks of illegal suppliers and dealers that are difficult to control.

Drug traders are often involved in other illegal activities as well. Many of the people who buy and use the drugs get the money by illegal means

Most states say you must be 21 years old to drink alcohol.

Drugs and Your Rights

Many young people are involved with drugs. Some use drugs themselves. Some sell drugs to others. You may have been offered drugs. You may know someone who uses them. Drugs are one of the biggest sources of trouble in schools today.

To fight the drug problem, many schools conduct searches of lockers and people's clothing. Many people feel that these searches violate students' rights.

The Bill of Rights protects us from *illegal searches and seizures.* This means that the police or your school principal cannot look for drugs in your pockets or your locker whenever they choose. For a search to be legal, they must have strong reasons to believe that you are concealing drugs.

You, Drugs, and Your Parents

When your parents are involved, the idea of illegal searches and seizures does not apply. Your right not to be searched does not include the right not to be searched by your parents. Their parental right to protect and care for you allows them to legally search your clothes, your room, or anything else .

It is far better for parents and children to be able to deal with these issues in an atmosphere of trust. When it comes to questions about drugs, your parents should be able to trust you to carry out the responsibilities that go along with your rights.

Chapter 9

Gerald and the Juvenile Justice System

*G*erald and his friend Ronnie called Mrs. Cook *on the telephone and said some "dirty" words to her. Mrs. Cook called the police. The police were able to find out that the call came from Gerald's house. They went there and found Gerald and Ronnie. They took them to a juvenile detention center. A juvenile detention center is a place where young people are kept when they are arrested by the police.*

The next day a juvenile court judge had a hearing about Gerald. Juvenile courts handle cases involving young people. They are a separate system from the courts and judges for adults. The judge asked Gerald questions. Mrs. Cook was not there.

A few days later there was a second hearing. The judge decided that Gerald must go to the state industrial training school. He would have to stay there until he reached his majority.

An industrial training school is not a regular school. It is actually a type of jail for young people. Majority is the age at which a person legally becomes an adult. In most states an 18-year-old is considered an adult. Gerald was 15.

Gerald's parents spent three years going to other courts trying to get Gerald free. Finally, the Supreme Court decided that Gerald's parents were right. By that time, Gerald had become 18.

If you believe any of your legal rights have been violated, you can seek the advice of a lawyer.

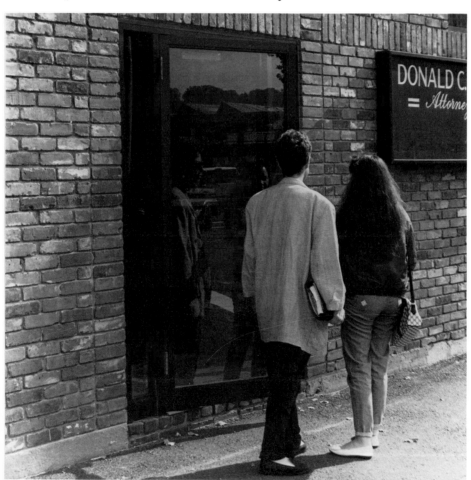

Gerald and the Supreme Court

What happened to Gerald is a true story. Gerald's full name is Gerald Gault.

The Supreme Court said that Gerald was prevented from exercising his rights. A person who is arrested has several rights.

- The right to be considered innocent until proved otherwise.
- The right to be represented by a lawyer.
- If the arrested person cannot pay a lawyer, the government must provide one.
- The right to refuse to answer any questions that may *incriminate*—make the person seem guilty.
- The right to see the people who say you broke the law and to ask them any questions.

Since Gerald won his case, things have changed a great deal. If you are arrested today and brought before a judge, you have the right to be represented by a lawyer. The police and the judge must prove that you did the things you are accused of doing. They must let your lawyer try to prove that you did *not* do what the police claim you did.

You can *appeal* the decision of the judge. In an appeal, you ask a second judge to determine whether mistakes were made at your trial and whether your rights were restricted or denied.

The law provides citizens with many rights if they are arrested or taken into custody.

Chapter 10

The Juvenile Justice System and You

T here are two ways in which you can become involved with the juvenile justice system. The first is to be *taken into custody* for breaking the law. Being taken into custody means that a police officer or court officer takes you to a juvenile detention center. There they indicate what crime you have been accused of.

Being taken into custody is like being arrested. The difference is that you can be taken without proof if a police officer or court officer *thinks* you have done something wrong.

In many cases, if the young people who were taken into custody had been treated the way adults are treated, they could not have been arrested. Why not? Because there was not enough evidence to prove they had committed crimes.

You can also be brought into the juvenile justice system if you cannot control how you act and your parents are no longer able to help you control yourself. In some states you would be referred to as a *Person In Need of Supervision* (PINS for short).

The most common reasons young people are considered in need of supervision are (1) being repeatedly absent from school, (2) running away from home, and (3) constantly fighting with their parents. You do not have to break a specific law or commit a crime to become a PINS.

How the Juvenile Justice System May Treat You

If you are taken into the system, you have the right to *due process*. Due process is a legal term meaning that all of your rights must be respected. These include your right to be represented by a lawyer and your right to know the exact reasons why you have been brought in. These rights are discussed in Chapter 9.

If a judge decides something must be done about you, there are three kinds of action she or he can order. The first is *probation*. Probation is a legal term meaning that you will be supervised by an officer of the court for a specific period of time. The officers are called *probation officers*. The period of time might be as short as six months or as long as two or three years.

If you are on probation you must meet regularly with a probation officer. Usually you will agree to certain things that the officer thinks are necessary.

The second type of action the judge might order is that you attend a special school. Sometimes these are called industrial training schools, the type Gerald Gault was sent to in Arizona. Sometimes they are called *reform schools*. These schools are basically prisons, but they do provide courses like ordinary schools. The doors are locked, however, and the outdoor areas are fenced in.

Being Tried as an Adult

The third type of action the judge can order is that you be tried as an adult. When this happens, your case is transferred to a regular judge of the criminal court system. You may have a trial, or you may arrange a *plea bargain*. In a plea bargain, the person charged with committing a crime agrees to admit being guilty. The judge responds by ordering a less severe punishment.

The number of young people tried as adults has been increasing steadily. Most of these young people have committed very serious crimes. For example, if a young person kills someone with a gun, he or she will probably be tried as an adult. A young person who is heavily involved in drug dealing can also be tried by the courts as an adult.

If someone is tried as a juvenile, the judge cannot order a sentence that continues beyond age 21.

Rosa Parks helped to spark the civil rights movement of the 1960s. In Alabama in 1955, she refused to give up her seat on a bus to a white person.

Chapter 11

Things *Can* Change

January 15 is the day Americans honor Dr. Martin Luther King, Jr. for his accomplishments as a leader of the *civil rights movement* in the United States. The civil rights movement was a struggle to make sure that all people can fully exercise their rights. Age, sex, race, or religion cannot be the reason for treating any one person differently from another.

The struggle for American civil rights began in colonial times. On July 4, Americans celebrate the adoption of the Declaration of Independence in 1776. The Declaration was another important part of the struggle for our rights. On Presidents' Day, in February, Americans honor George Washington and Abraham Lincoln. As the first president of the United States, Washington helped make sure that the Bill of Rights was added to the Constitution.

Abraham Lincoln was president of the United States during the Civil War. We remember him for helping to eliminate slavery. After the Civil War, important amendments were added to the Constitution. These amendments made slavery illegal, gave ex-slaves the right to vote, and guaranteed all U.S. citizens equal protection under the law.

First Blacks, Then Women, Then Young People

Women have also been prevented from exercising their rights fully and equally. In the United States, the struggle for women to exercise their right to vote went on for almost a hundred years. Finally an amendment to the Constitution was passed guaranteeing that no one could prevent women from voting.

Soon after 1963, women began to realize that their rights were limited in many of the ways black people's rights were restricted. A new women's rights movement began.

An important part of the movement for young people's rights began with what happened to Gerald Gault. Gerald and his parents fought to get him the same rights adults have when they are arrested.

Another part of the movement involved freedom of speech. John Tinker, Mary Beth Tinker, and Christopher Eckhardt were high school students in Des Moines, Iowa. They wore black armbands to school to protest against the war in Vietnam.

After being shot in an assassination attempt in 1981, James Brady worked to strengthen laws against guns. In 1991, a gun-control measure—known as the Brady Bill— was finally approved by Congress.

Their principal suspended them from school until they gave up wearing the armbands. Like Gerald Gault, they appealed in the courts and finally reached the Supreme Court.

The Supreme Court said that their right to freedom of speech gave them the right to wear the armbands to school. As long as what they were doing did not interfere with classes, the principal could not suspend them.

Experts in legal rights often say that young people did not begin to be treated as people until the Supreme Court decided these two cases: the case of Gerald Gault and the case of the Tinkers and their friend. The Supreme Court said that young people have the same rights as adults. It said young people's exercise of their rights could be restricted. But they could not be treated as if they had no rights at all.

Back to the Beginnings and on to the Future

This brings us back to the question we discussed in the Introduction. What do your rights have to do with being right?

The answer is that your rights make it possible for you to do what you think is right. If someone tells you what you are doing is wrong, ask them to give you reasons. If you have to "fight city hall," or your school principal, get other kids to help you. Ask your parents to help you too.

Remember that rights come with responsibilities attached. You must show that you can act responsibly, you must respect other people's rights.

Remember also that our laws are always changing. As young people have shown that they can exercise their rights responsibly, the laws have been changed to allow them more freedom. You can keep this progress going. Other young people did it before you. Now it is your turn.

Glossary—*Explaining New Words*

abortion   A procedure that removes a developing ovum or "egg," ending a pregnancy.

abuse   Treating someone in a way that is cruel and harmful.

age of consent   Age at which young people may marry without parental permission; also age at which a young woman may legally agree to have sexual intercourse.

appeal   A procedure that allows a young person to take the decision of a juvenile court judge to another, higher court.

Bill of Rights   The proclamation of your most important rights and freedoms in the first ten amendments to the Constitution.

civil rights   The personal rights and freedoms of individuals.

custody   An official decision, by a judge, about who will be responsible for taking care of a child or a young person.

divorce   The legal ending of a marriage.

freedom of speech   Your right to say what you wish whenever and wherever you desire.

freedom of the press   Your right to print whatever you wish in a book, pamphlet, newspaper, or magazine.

industrial training school   A special school that supervises young people who have committed serious crimes.

juvenile court   A system of judges and officers who listen to complaints against young people.

juvenile detention center   Where young people are kept before they see a juvenile court judge.

lawyer   A person who legally practices law.

minimum wage   The lowest amount of money per hour that may be paid legally to a worker.

neglect   A failure to do the things one is required to do for another person.

nuisance   A thing or activity that interferes with someone's enjoyment, causes them physical discomfort, or makes them afraid they will be injured.

PINS   Person In Need of Supervision; a young person who cannot be controlled by his or her parents or teachers.

rape   Forcing a woman to have sexual intercourse against her will.

reform school   A school that supervises young people who have committed serious crimes.

rehabilitation   Enabling people to learn to control their behavior.

rights   Your basic freedom.

separation   A legal agreement between husband and wife to live apart.

Supreme Court   The highest court in the American legal system, made up of nine judges appointed by the President.

work permit   A document that allows a young person to work at a particular job.

Where to Get Help

If going to your parents is a problem, go to teachers you trust, your friends' parents, your school librarian, school nurse, or a minister, rabbi, or YWCA or YMCA leader you know and trust.

Local and State Agencies: Public Defender's Office, Legal Aid Society, Legal Assistance Association, state chapter or affiliate of the American Civil Liberties Union.

National Organizations:

National Juvenile Law Center
3701 Lindell Boulevard
P.O. Box 14200
St. Louis, MO 63178
(314) 652-5555

American Civil Liberties Union
Children's Rights Project
132 West 43rd St.
New York, NY 10036
(212) 944-9800

Youth Law Center
693 Mission St.
San Francisco, CA 94105

Children's Defense Fund
Legal Division
1520 New Hampshire Ave., NW
Washington, DC 20036
(202) 483-1470

NAACP Legal Defense Fund
10 Columbus Circle
New York, NY 10019
(212) 586-8397

For Further Reading

Atkinson, Linda. *Your Legal Rights.* New York, NY: Franklin Watts, 1982.

Berry, Joy. *Every Kid's Guide to the Juvenile Justice System.* Chicago, IL: Children's Press, 1987.

Guggenheim, Martin, and Alan Sussman. *The Rights of Young People.* An American Civil Liberties Handbook. New York, NY: Bantam Books, 1985.

Olney, Ross, and Patricia Olney. *Up Against the Law: Your Rights as a Minor.* New York, NY: Lodestar Books, 1986.

Price, Janet, and Alan Levine and Eve Cary. *The Rights of Students.* An American Civil Liberties Handbook. Southern Illinois University Press, 1988.

Sloan, Irving. *Youth and the Law.* Dobbs Ferry, NY: Oceana, 1981.

Index

About the Author
Kenneth Fox is an author and a university professor. He was co-director of the Washington Mini-School in Washington, D.C., an experimental program for sixth graders about government, the law, young people's rights, and making places for children in adult organizations. He has written on the law and American cities and on the history of American cities. He has taught history and public administration at the University of Massachusetts, Yale University, and Rutgers University.

Acknowledgements and Photo Credits
Cover photo by Chuck Peterson.
All photographs by Stuart Rabinowitz, except page 2, Chris Volpe; page 50, ©Jean Marc Giboux/Gamma Liaison; pages 54, 57, Wide World Photos.

Design/Production: Blackbirch Graphics, Inc.